MW01257952

Headless
at
Halloween

NIGHTMARE
ARIZONA
PARANORMAL COZY MYSTERIES

BETH DOLGNER

Headless at Halloween
A Nightmare, Arizona Paranormal Cozy Mysteries Novella
© 2024 Beth Dolgner

All rights reserved. No portion of this book may be reproduced in any form without permission from the publisher, except as permitted by U.S. copyright law.

Print ISBN-13: 978-1-958587-25-6

Headless at Halloween is a work of fiction. Names, characters, places, and incidents either are the products of the author's imagination or are used fictitiously. Any resemblance to actual persons, living or dead, businesses, companies, events, or locales is entirely coincidental.

Published by Redglare Press
Cover by Dark Mojo Designs
Print Formatting by The Madd Formatter

https://bethdolgner.com

CHAPTER ONE

"Free books!" I said happily.

The librarian laughed. "Yes, as long as you bring them back on time and don't have to pay a late fee!"

I tilted the orange laminated card back and forth, its shiny surface reflecting the bright overhead lights. I had never had much time for reading when I lived in Nashville. My life there had been all about my career and trying to fit in with the well-off people around me. Here in Nightmare, I had more interest in good books than in heading to the latest trendy restaurant.

"Thank you," I told the librarian. "I'm going to go pick out a book or two now."

"You're most welcome. I've got to pop down to the basement to bring up the rest of the Halloween decorations, so if I'm not here when you get back, just sit tight for a moment or two." The librarian gave her short gray hair a little pat, and her eyebrows rose dramatically behind her bright-yellow reading glasses. "But if you hear me scream, it means the basement monster got me!"

I smiled. "I work with monsters every day," I assured her. The librarian, of course, had no idea I meant it literally. "If anything happens, my friends and I will come to your rescue."

As I was turning away from the worn mahogany counter, a man took my place and plunked a book down.

The librarian had been joking with me, but her tone suddenly turned wary. "A book about malpractice law?"

"Not so loud, Renee!" the man said in a loud whisper. "And none of your business."

"Doc, I've been going to you for thirty years. It is my business!"

I had paused to eavesdrop on the conversation, and I threw what I hoped was a clandestine look over my shoulder. The man appeared to be in his late fifties or early sixties, and he had a bushy white beard that made him look more like Santa Claus than a doctor.

His face must get awfully hot here in the desert.

If I continued to stand there, it would be obvious I was listening in, so I began to walk in the direction of the nearest row of books. As I went, I heard the doctor hiss, "It's no big deal, Renee. I'm just doing some research. You know I'm a good physician."

Renee's response was too low for me to hear as I entered the quiet of the row. I wanted something spooky to fit with the Halloween season, and I was searching for something by one of my favorite authors. I relished running my fingers lightly over the spines of the books, and I inhaled deeply as I appreciated the distinct smell of printed pages.

I picked a book, and just as I exited the row, I bumped into Justine and Clara. We had driven to the Nightmare Public Library together, agreeing we all needed a bit of an escape from work.

Not that I disliked my job. In fact, I didn't think I had ever been happier, even back when I had made big bucks and driven a fancy car. Working at Nightmare Sanctuary Haunted House felt like coming home every time I walked through the front doors of the former hospital building. If someone had told teenage me that I would someday work at a year-round haunted house attraction—and that I would love it—I would have laughed.

"Olivia, you must be joking," Justine said. She peered at my selection over the stack of books in her arms. "Thousands of books to choose from, and you went for a murder mystery?"

"It's by one of my favorite authors, and it seems like an appropriate choice for Halloween."

Clara giggled, the high sound almost musical. "We just had to deal with Annabelle's murder less than a week ago, and now you want more?"

"Sure, why not?" I asked in mock innocence. "I can pretend it's research, so I'm better prepared the next time a dead body shows up in this town."

"There weren't this many murders before you arrived in Nightmare," Justine said thoughtfully.

"So Officer Reyes tells me," I said, rolling my eyes. Reyes was a good police officer, and he and I usually bumped into each other whenever I poked my nose into a local murder case.

I was pretty sure he was getting tired of me and my nose.

As we walked toward the counter to check out our books, Clara yawned widely. She gave her body a little shake, her silvery hair dancing around her shoulders. The movement briefly exposed the pointed tips of her fairy ears. "I'm going to need a cup of coffee or a nap before I start reading."

"You just got up a couple of hours ago," Justine reminded her. It was well after noon, but working at a haunted house that was open late meant most of my friends kept unusual hours. So did I, for that matter.

Halloween was only two days away. Work had been busy the entire month of October, but the last few days had been almost overwhelming. People wanting to get into the spirit were lining up as much as two hours before we opened each evening, and we were staying open an hour later than usual. That meant I wasn't getting off work until one o'clock every night.

Er, morning. I still wasn't sure how to think of it.

We were all tired but pleased with the flood of guests coming through the haunt and the resulting income for the Sanctuary. Things would calm down after Halloween, and we could all get caught up on sleep.

We had just reached the countertop when Justine stopped. "I almost forgot! I told Mori I'd get her a book. Be right back!" She headed off toward a row of books, her wavy chestnut hair bobbing in time with her steps.

The librarian—Renee, the doctor had called her—wasn't at the counter, which meant she had made a run to the basement. As Clara and I waited for both her and Justine to return, we suddenly heard Justine calling to us in a whisper.

"Come here," she said. Since she had an armload of books, she jerked her head toward an area behind her.

When Clara and I got closer, Justine smiled. "The library has set up a little haunt of their own! Let's go through it before we check out!"

"Will there be a beautiful fairy inside it?" Clara asked with a grin. She batted her eyelashes, her violet eyes shining.

"There will be once you go in!" Justine teased.

The library's version of a haunted attraction began with a tattered curtain across one row of books, and a sign next to it read *Enter if you dare!* We put our books down on a nearby table, then went through the curtain, giggling. Since we were in a library, we made sure it was quiet giggling.

Black plastic—it looked like garbage bags to me—

across the top of the row made the scene relatively dark as we stepped into the makeshift haunt. There were fake cobwebs arrayed across rows of books, a plastic skeleton lying on an empty shelf, and a short stretch that had fake arms sticking out from the shelves, requiring us to weave our way carefully past them.

The haunt was clearly made for young kids. And, as someone who had always avoided walking through haunted attractions because they were too scary, I decided the library's haunted house was right up my alley. On the nights I was stationed in one of the scenes inside the Sanctuary, instead of taking tickets at the door, I loved scaring guests. I just didn't like to be on the receiving end of getting scared.

We reached the end of the row and went through another tattered curtain. I was the last one to come out, and as the curtain fell back into place behind me, we heard a distinct scream.

"Wow," Clara said. "I'm surprised they have sound effects in the haunt, since this is a library. Shouldn't the monsters be whispering, too?"

"I don't think the scream was coming from the haunt," Justine said slowly. She had tensed up, and she leaned forward as she listened intently.

There was another scream, and it was clear it wasn't coming from a hidden speaker somewhere behind us.

Immediately, all three of us began to hurry toward the counter, our books forgotten for the time being. The sound had come from that direction, but when we arrived, there was no one to be seen. I looked around, and I saw a few other people peeking out from between rows of books, their faces showing a mixture of confusion and alarm.

There was an open door behind the counter. "Through there, maybe?" I suggested, already moving in that direction.

Before I could reach the doorway, though, Renee came running out of it. Her chest was heaving, and her cheeks were red. She stopped when she saw us, gasping for breath. "Downstairs…" she said.

"What happened?" I asked, reaching an arm toward her. Renee's eyes had a slightly glazed look, and I was worried she might faint.

"There's a body! In the basement!"

CHAPTER TWO

Renee grabbed my hand, and Justine jumped forward to help me lead her to a nearby chair. Once she was seated, Renee began to recover. Her breathing slowed down a little, and after shutting her eyes tightly for a moment, she looked more clear-sighted when she gazed up at us again.

"Tell us what happened," I said gently.

"We store all of our Halloween decorations down there," Renee said, gesturing in the direction of the door she had come through. "I've been bringing things up here and there, but the big pieces need to come out for our Halloween reading party on Saturday."

Renee stopped and hitched in a breath. Tears were clearly not far off, and Clara made soothing noises to try to calm Renee down.

"If you've been making trips to the basement all month," I said, "then that must mean someone only recently died down there."

Renee shook her head, then took off her glasses and wiped at her eyes. "I don't know how long he's been down there. I was dusting off the prop coffin, and when I opened the lid, I saw him inside."

Justine tilted her head slightly. She started to speak, stopped, then tried again. "Maybe," she said, clearly choosing her words with care, "the body was a prop, too. We work at Nightmare Sanctuary Haunted House, and we all know what it's like to be startled by a dummy."

Renee was shaking her head before Justine had even finished. "No. This was a body." She even looked slightly offended as she looked at Justine. "I think I know a dead body when I see one."

"Why don't you show us?" I asked. I couldn't imagine who would dump a dead body in the basement of a library, so I was inclined to side with Justine. Renee probably saw a prop, and her imagination had run with it. There was no point calling the police until we knew for sure what was really inside the coffin.

Renee stood up and took a long, slow breath. "Okay, but I'm not going to look at it again." She walked, almost on tiptoe, through the doorway, as if she were afraid she might disturb the body somewhere below us.

The alleged body, I reminded myself.

The basement stairs were on the left, just after passing through the doorway, and I was happy to see they were proper stairs, rather than the narrow, rickety kind that always made me feel like I was descending into a horror movie. The basement wasn't well-lit, but it was brighter than I had anticipated, and I began to doubt myself for doubting Renee. The basement wasn't a creepy place with looming shadows or damp corners, so I didn't think she had simply let the place get to her imagination.

Renee stopped at the bottom of the stairs and pressed her back against the concrete wall. "That way," she said, gesturing toward the far corner. "All of our Halloween stuff is over there. I'll wait here."

Somehow, I wound up at the front of the group. Clara and Justine were close behind me, though, as I crossed to the other side of the basement and spotted the prop coffin. It looked like it was made of plywood, and it had been painted to resemble planks of pine. It sat on top of a row of plastic storage bins, which were all labeled *Halloween.*

The lid of the coffin was closed, and I was surprised how much trepidation I felt as I reached out a hand to open it. My fingers were even shaking.

I got exactly two inches of the lid open before an acrid smell reached my nostrils, and I instinctively dropped the lid and pressed my hand over my nose.

"That," I said in a slightly nasal voice, "is not a prop."

"Agreed," Justine said. She had lifted the neck of her black Nightmare Sanctuary T-shirt to cover her mouth and nose. "But let's see what we're dealing with before we call the police."

In that moment, I knew Justine was a braver person than I was. She stepped up next to me and lifted the coffin lid all the way while I took a step back.

The smell was stronger with the lid open but not nearly as bad as I had expected. Inside, as Renee had said, was a man's body. He was wearing a flamboyant blue floral-print shirt and green cargo shorts, looking like he ought to be on vacation in Hawaii rather than lying dead in a basement.

What Renee had not said was that the body didn't have a head. Instead, there was a plastic jack-o'-lantern where the man's head should have been. It seemed to be grinning right at me.

"Ugh," I mumbled, my hand still pressed against my face. "Let's get out of here."

We did just that, walking silently as we headed up the basement stairs and back into the brightness of the library. Justine volunteered to call the police as Clara escorted Renee to the chair again. That left me to do a little crowd control. There was a cluster of people at the counter, all looking eager to find out what was going on.

"I'm so sorry," I told them. "The library is going to have to close early."

"What happened?" a woman asked, staring at Renee with open curiosity.

"We're not sure yet," I hedged.

"Is she going to pass out?" This time, it was a man who was talking. "I know CPR!"

Despite the grim situation, I nearly laughed. "That's great, but if anyone does faint, they won't need CPR."

There was some grumbling among the assembled people as they realized I wasn't going to say a word about what we'd seen in the basement. I just shrugged it off. Nightmare residents loved gossip, so of course, they were disappointed with me.

They'll find out soon enough, I thought.

I was a little surprised Renee hadn't mentioned the part about the body being headless, though I supposed she was in so much shock that she had forgotten to relay that little detail. Or, maybe, the whole thing had happened so quickly she hadn't even registered the toothy jack-o'-lantern smile.

I pondered that and other details while we waited for the police to arrive. The people at the counter were still waiting expectantly, though they dutifully stepped to one side as four police officers approached.

Luis Reyes gave an audible sigh as he walked up to me. "How is it," he asked me in an undertone, "that you're already on the case?"

I raised my hands defensively. "We just happened to be here when Renee found the body. Besides, we don't even know it was murder."

Reyes nodded in Justine's direction. He was already acquainted with both her and Clara from previous murder investigations. "Ms. Abbott reported that the man has no head. I don't think that counts as natural causes."

Oh, right.

Reyes spoke briefly with Renee, who relayed how she

had made the discovery. When she was done, Reyes looked around at the other officers and said, "Let's go take a look."

He hadn't invited Justine, Clara, and me to join him, but we followed, anyway.

Soon, I was in the basement again, but this time, I stayed well back from the plywood coffin. We watched silently as the police took a look, and at some point, Renee crept up beside us. Clara gave her a comforting pat on the back.

"Being a librarian isn't supposed to involve dead bodies," Renee said in a flat voice.

Reyes turned toward us, and his reddish-brown eyes were thoughtful as he asked, "None of you recognize him?"

"He's missing his head," I said. *Talk about pointing out the obvious.*

"Yes, but I thought you might recognize the clothing. Unfortunately, there's no form of identification on him."

I pursed my lips and looked in the direction of the coffin. "Do you think the killer took his wallet so he wouldn't be easy to ID?"

Reyes shook his head slightly. "Maybe. Taking the wallet and the head makes it much harder to identify the body. There's no face for someone to recognize, and no teeth to compare to dental records. But why would anyone go to such lengths to hide the victim's identity, then leave the body in a place it would inevitably be found?"

"And," Justine piped up, "was the guy killed down here, or somewhere else? And if he was killed somewhere else, then why did the killer decide to come here to stash the body?"

"In my library," Renee added. Her voice was sounding stronger, I noticed.

"Good questions," Reyes said. "We've got a lot of work

to do. You know, Halloween crime is usually limited to trespassers at the abandoned hotel, not murder." He looked at me significantly. "But, of course, now that you're in town, Ms. Kendrick…"

"Yes, I know, you say there weren't this many murders before I got here three months ago." I could hear the edge of annoyance in my tone, but I didn't feel bad about that at all. Reyes seemed to think I was somehow responsible for the dead bodies that kept showing up in Nightmare. "Plus, I thought we were on a first-name basis now?"

"Yes, Olivia, we are."

"Also, there's an abandoned hotel around here?"

Reyes raised a finger toward me. "Don't even think about it. That place is off limits. It may not be structurally sound anymore, and it's on private property."

The way Reyes was lecturing me almost made me laugh. Only remembering why we were both standing in the library basement kept me quiet.

"We'll get everything cordoned off and begin our investigation," Reyes said to Renee. "We'll have more questions for you, of course."

"Of course," Renee echoed. She was the first one to start heading up the stairs. I was right behind her, but as I lifted my foot to take the first step, I saw a flash of light on the ground, just a few feet away. It was a library card, its laminated surface reflecting the overhead light, just as mine had done. Except this one was more of a dull shine, and when I stepped closer, I could see the card was covered with a fine layer of dust.

"Someone dropped their library card down here," I said, bending at the waist to pick it up.

"Wait!" Reyes called. To add emphasis to his command, he gently put his hand on my arm as he stepped up next to me.

"But only staff comes down here," Renee said.

Reyes had pulled a small flashlight off his belt, and he shined it down at the library card. "*Pete Bennett*," he read.

Renee gasped. "Pete Bennett? He's that old curmudgeon who always wore the tackiest Hawaiian shirts."

"Well," I said, "I think we know who's in the coffin."

CHAPTER THREE

"The killer must have dropped it," Reyes noted. He glanced up at the staircase, then down to where Pete Bennett's library card was collecting dust. "If the killer had the victim's wallet in their hand, the library card might have slipped out as they started up the stairs."

"Judging by the dust, that card has been here for a while," I noted.

Reyes gave me an appreciative look. "Well done, Olivia. And judging by the state of the body, it's been here for a while, too."

"That part I did *not* notice." I scrunched up my nose. I had gotten a sniff but not a good look at Pete.

"Ms. Porter," Reyes said, looking up to where Renee was leaning over the staircase railing, "when was the last time you saw Pete Bennett alive?"

"Oh, it's been months," Renee said without hesitation. "He returned his last books in April, and I figured he'd gone north for the summer, like he always did." She gave a visible shudder. "And to think, he's been dead in my basement this whole time!"

"We don't know how long he's been here," Reyes pointed out, "but I assure you, we'll find out. Do you know if Pete had any enemies? I believe you referred to the victim just now as a curmudgeon."

Renee gave a little sniff. "I stand by what I said. I hate to speak ill of the dead, but you'd be hard pressed to find anyone in Nightmare with something good to say about Pete. I know the public library is for everyone in the community, but he was the one person I really wanted to ban from coming in here."

"Why?" I asked, surprised.

"He was the meanest old man. Never a kind word for anybody, and always threatening to *have our jobs* anytime he couldn't get things his way. He once complained that he couldn't find the book he wanted, and I told him that was because it was a popular book, and there was a waiting list. He insisted on being put at the top of the list, and when I said he'd have to wait his turn, just like everyone else, he wrote a letter to the mayor, demanding better of the library. He even called me out by name."

Pete didn't sound like a nice guy, by any means, but sending a whiny letter to the mayor of Nightmare certainly didn't seem like a motive for murder.

"This library card is a good start, but we'll want to get a more formal identification before we can say for sure that's who is in the coffin." Reyes looked at me sternly. "Meaning don't go telling anyone that Pete Bennett was found dead in the library basement."

I frowned at Reyes. "I'm not a Nightmare gossip queen," I reminded him.

"No, you're not. But it doesn't matter," Reyes muttered. He glanced up the stairs, and I knew he must be thinking of the people who would still be waiting at the counter. "Half this town will know the news before dinnertime."

I wished Reyes luck before leaving with Justine and Clara. He and I weren't exactly friends, and I was a bit rankled by his implication that I'd be spreading gossip, but I still wanted him to get to the bottom of what had happened.

Justine was driving, and it was only as she turned onto the main two-lane road that led through the old copper mining town of Nightmare that I realized we had forgotten all about the books we had selected. *Oh, well.* I had wanted a murder mystery but not like this.

Nightmare Sanctuary wouldn't open for nearly three hours, but I had already made plans with my boss, Damien Shackleford, to meet up with him beforehand. He was only beginning to explore his supernatural abilities, but so far, we weren't quite sure what he was capable of. What we did know was that he wasn't very good at controlling his psychic power on the occasions it did manifest. I was still learning how to be a conjuror, and lately, Damien and I were practicing together. It was more fun to work on our supernatural skills as a team.

There was one aspect, though, that wasn't fun. Damien had to get upset in order for his power to manifest. When his emotions were heightened, so was his ability. That meant we had to try to get him upset enough to trigger his power, but not so upset he might accidentally blow up his office with the power of his mind.

Well, it wasn't quite that extreme. No breakable dishes were safe in Damien's presence, at any rate.

There were still plenty of times that I couldn't quite believe I had landed not just in the middle of nowhere, Arizona, but that I was surrounded by supernatural creatures. It was even harder for me to believe I was one of them, but after everything I'd been through in the few short months I'd been in Nightmare, I had to admit I was definitely developing my skills as a conjuror. When I focused very intently on a specific outcome, I could make it happen.

Maybe someday I'd learn how to conjure myself a beachfront home and a life of luxury.

If that was ever going to happen, though, I would have to keep practicing.

Soon, Justine was pulling her car into the staff section of the parking area to one side of Nightmare Sanctuary Haunted House. It was really just a bare stretch of land, and as I glanced around on our walk to the building, I realized there were already a few cars in the guest section of the parking lot.

"People are really excited about Halloween," I noted as we approached the building. The weathered gray stone structure loomed above us, though in the daylight, the Sanctuary didn't look nearly as spooky as it did at night.

"Wait until the actual day of Halloween," Justine said. "Last year, we had a few people who set up grills out in the parking lot."

"They tailgated? Like before a football game?" I asked, surprised.

"We're the most popular spot in Nightmare on Halloween," Clara pointed out.

When we went through the double front doors of the Sanctuary, I turned right to head down the hallway that led to Damien's office. Clara and Justine both drifted upstairs. The old hospital rooms up there had been combined and renovated into small apartments, and both women lived there. In fact, most of my friends in Nightmare lived upstairs, meaning they all had a commute to work that was exactly one staircase long.

Damien's office door was closed when I approached, and when I knocked, there was no answer. I had raised my hand to knock a second time when I heard his voice behind me. "I thought we could practice in the dining room today."

I turned to see Damien wearing a gray suit with a burgundy button-down shirt. His dark-blond hair looked immaculate, as always. "You're awfully dressed up for practice," I noted.

Damien gave me a small smile. "I'm usually dressed like this."

"True." I fell into step next to Damien as we made our way to the dining room. "Did you hear about the murder?"

Damien hadn't, so I filled him in. When I was done, he just shook his head. "You do have a knack for running into dead people."

We had reached the dining room, and when Damien opened the door to let me inside, something darted out of it. I tried to avoid colliding with the rust-red blur heading toward me, but there wasn't enough time or space for me to do so.

"Oh!" I flailed my arms as the form hit me hard against my thighs and abdomen, and Damien deftly reached out and grabbed one of my hands to keep me from toppling over. "Zach!"

Zach looked up at me with a snort, seeming to imply that I was at fault for the collision. I could have been wrong in that assessment, though. It wasn't easy to read a were-wolf's expressions, at least during the three days a month they were in their wolf form.

"Zach, next time, look before you run through a door, please," Damien said tersely. He sounded like he was lecturing the family dog rather than the Sanctuary's accountant.

Zach huffed out a breath, then shook himself, his fur fluffing with the movement. Then, with one more glance at me, he padded down the hallway.

Damien was still holding my hand, and he dropped it as I cautiously tried going through the door again. This time, no supernatural creatures got in my way. Damien had just said I had a knack for running into dead people, but apparently, I had a knack for running into things in general.

I had expected to find the huge dining room empty, so I was surprised to see Malcolm sitting at one of the wooden tables that were lined up in rows. He was turned sideways, his long legs up on the bench and a book that looked older than him in his hands. Malcolm's black top hat sat on the table beside him.

"Hey, Malcolm," I called as he looked up.

"I thought Zach was going to knock you over," Malcolm answered calmly as he closed his book with a snap. "How are you today, Olivia?"

"We just found a dead body at the library," I said bluntly. For the second time in just a few minutes, I had to relay our adventure in the library basement.

"Pete Bennett?" Malcolm repeated when I had finished. He tilted his head thoughtfully, his thin, almost skeletal face pale in the sunlight streaming through the large windows along one wall. "He's got a reputation in this town. Most of the retired folks who winter in Nightmare are nice enough, but Pete is known for having a chip on his shoulder."

"Well, he doesn't have a head on his shoulders, that's for sure," I quipped.

"Strange." Malcolm touched a long finger to his bald head. "Removing the head is usually done to keep the body from being identified easily, but if the killer was trying to cover their tracks, why leave the body in the library basement?"

"That's our question, as well."

"And, if the head has been removed," Malcolm continued, "where is it? Did the killer bury it in the desert somewhere? Keep it as a trophy?"

"Ew." I wrinkled my nose.

"I could have probably identified Pete just by smell. He had a distinct odor."

Again, I wrinkled my nose. Not because I was remembering what Pete had smelled like, but because I knew Malcolm was a fierce supernatural predator. It was one of the reasons he was so good at sniffing out humans. Malcolm was a really good guy, and it was easy to forget he had once been even more dangerous than whomever had murdered Pete.

I heard the door squeak, and I turned to see Seraphina and Fiona coming into the room. Fiona was pushing Seraphina's mobile water tank. It slightly resembled a barrel on wheels, and Seraphina's back was pressed against one side, while her silver siren's tail curled up out of the water on the opposite side.

Seraphina sat up a little straighter when she saw us. "We were hoping to find you here, Olivia! Justine just told us there was a murder at the library."

"Pete Bennett," Malcolm said. "The meanest old man in Nightmare."

"That's who it was?" Fiona asked, her dark eyes wide. She leaned slightly forward, sending her long black hair falling over her shoulders. "I thought he'd just gone north for the summer! I used to see him out for early-morning walks sometimes. Whenever I tried to be friendly and say hello, he would always scowl at me."

"He seems to have been universally disliked," I noted.

"Even his wife disliked him," Fiona said. "Sometimes, she would be out walking with him, and I would be able to hear her telling him how awful he was all the way from my spot on the other side of the street. I figured if one of them was going to die, it would be him murdering her!"

CHAPTER FOUR

Malcolm made a dismissive gesture. "It's hard to believe anyone wanted to marry that guy, but I can believe his wife would have wanted to murder him."

"I wonder if the police are going to consider Pete's wife as a suspect," I mused. Would she be sad to hear the news of Pete's demise? Or did she already know because she had done it?

"I expect the wife was gone all summer, too." Fiona shrugged. "Though you'd think she would have reported him missing."

"Maybe she did," Damien pointed out. "But, from what Olivia has said, the body has been there for a while, so the police may not have been actively looking for Pete anymore."

"Or, maybe," I countered, "she didn't report him missing, because she's the one who killed him."

We speculated for a few more minutes, but finally, I shook my head firmly. "It's not our business, anyway. Like Clara pointed out when we were at the library, we all just got past Annabelle's murder, and we don't need to get involved in another investigation."

"Especially at Halloween," Seraphina said, nodding. "We've got enough going on."

Damien was peering at me with his green eyes, his lips

clamped firmly together. He was clearly trying not to laugh.

"What?" I asked.

"You're saying 'we,' but I get the impression you're trying to talk yourself out of diving into this case."

"Well…"

I was spared from having to find a suitable response by Justine, who came into the room just then. Damien turned to her and said, "I was going to come find you after practicing with Olivia. We've got a few props that might need some repair work before Halloween. Can you please go check the coffin in the mausoleum vignette?"

As one, we all groaned.

"Really?" Justine asked, rolling her eyes toward the ceiling. "After what we went through this morning, I'm not checking anything that's made for storing dead bodies. Even if it's just a prop."

"I'll check," Malcolm said, rising gracefully. "My day could use a little excitement."

"Be careful what you wish for," Justine cautioned as he headed toward the door.

"Hopefully, we'll have a little excitement, too," Damien said. He gestured out the nearest window. "Olivia, let's go out back to practice. It's a little too crowded in here for it."

Damien and I often tried practicing our supernatural skills outside, where he was less likely to break or damage something if he gave off a big burst of psychic power. Unfortunately, he hadn't been able to do that lately, because getting him upset enough to unleash his power was easier said than done.

Still, we gave it our best shot. Damien and I went out into the Sanctuary's backyard and picked a spot underneath a cluster of palo verde trees. Damien shut his eyes and thought about whatever it was that made him upset—he'd never told me, but I suspected a lot of the thoughts had to do with his ex-fiancée—while I stood ready to dive out of the way if he started to show signs of unleashing his psychic power. The last thing I wanted was for Damien to throw a tree branch in my face with the power of his mind.

In fact, while Damien did his own work, I focused on conjuring my safety. *I will not be hit by any flying objects,* I repeated to myself.

After an hour, we were both about ready to give up. Damien was annoyed and disappointed with himself, and I was simply bored.

I was staring at Damien's face, looking for any signs of heightened emotions, when I heard the distinct sound of paws against the hard-packed dirt nearby.

"Zach," I warned quietly as I turned toward the sound.

But it wasn't Zach. It was Felipe, Mori's pet chupacabra. He trotted up to us, his tail wagging and his tongue lolling out below his gray leathery snout.

I lifted one finger to my lips, since Damien still had his eyes closed in concentration, and Felipe sat down on his haunches, watching us. Damien, though, had also heard his approach, and he opened his eyes. They were glowing faintly, a sign that his emotions were, in fact, heightened.

They just weren't heightened enough to trigger his power.

"Let's call it a day," he said, already turning to go back inside.

"Not yet," I said, waving toward the trail that led to the old hospital cemetery. "You should walk it off."

Damien grimaced. "Do I look that miserable?"

"It's your eyes, mostly. Plus, I know this isn't easy for you. I hate that practicing involves making you upset."

Damien looked at Felipe. "Hey, boy, want to walk with us?"

Felipe hopped up onto his hind legs and made a snuffling noise.

Damien was mostly silent as we walked the trail that wound through scrubby trees and low bushes, and it wasn't until we reached the cemetery's rusted iron fence that he said, "You should keep looking into this murder."

I didn't know what I had expected Damien to say, but it was definitely not that. "Oh?" I said, too surprised to say anything else.

"You're trying to grow your skills as a conjuror, and this murder is a good chance for you to work on them. Focus on how much you want to find resolution to Pete's death. Conjure success for the police, or conjure suspects to talk to. Something that will give you a chance to grow your abilities."

I nodded slowly as I opened the gate in the fence. The hinges squealed loudly, and Felipe gave a little yip of displeasure. I walked thoughtfully until I finally stopped in front of a worn headstone for someone who had died in 1882.

"I'll try," I agreed. "But Fiona was right: we have our hands full here with Halloween crowds. Maybe I can conjure easy clues!"

Damien laughed. "Right. The clues will throw themselves at your feet, and you won't have to lift a finger."

"That's what I want," I said, beginning to walk again. "When I'm not scaring people tonight, I'll focus on how much I desire easy clues."

The bit of humor seemed to drain the last of Damien's angst, and we spent the rest of our walk talking easily. Felipe scampered among the graves, eventually disappearing through a gap in the fence. I wasn't worried, because I knew he could take care of himself. Plus, since I had arrived in Nightmare, I'd only heard one report about Felipe sneaking out and wreaking havoc on the local cow population.

There was still plenty of time before that night's family

meeting, when Justine would fill the staff in on anything important and assign roles to those of us who tended to float between positions. I decided to take a cue from Malcolm, and after selecting a book about the history of Nightmare from Damien's office, I settled onto a bench in the dining room to read.

The time went by quickly, and soon, the room around me began to fill up. Theo and Mori, the two vampires who usually sat with me for the family meeting, came in shortly after the sky outside the windows had darkened.

"Malcolm just told me the news," Theo said in greeting. He hadn't yet put on his zombie makeup, so I could appreciate just how handsome he was without it. He smiled widely at me, though there were no long fangs to give away the fact he was a vampire. A slayer had seen to that, filing them down so Theo could no longer feed from humans.

Not directly, anyway. Theo got around the issue by using a small knife. He would mesmerize a person, make a small cut so he could drink their blood, then send them on their way with no memory of what had just happened. Tourists were constantly coming through Nightmare, so Theo and Mori always had new people to feed from, and the residents of Nightmare had no idea what was going on in their own town.

"A new week, a new murder," I told Theo sarcastically.

He laughed, his brown eyes glittering. "You see more dead bodies than I do, and I'm a vampire!"

"But you only drink from living people," I pointed out.

"True. I once got desperate and drank from a dead man." Theo made a retching noise. "I was sick for days afterward."

"Gross."

"It was back in my pirate days. We were stuck at sea for

weeks because the wind had died, and I was starving. I didn't want to feed from the crew, but—"

I was spared the gory details by Mori, who had been listening to our exchange silently. She lifted a hand. "No, Theo," she said in a firm tone. "You will make me sick for days, too, if you get into details."

"You highfalutin ladies are always so sensitive," Theo teased.

Mori just pursed her lips in response. She couldn't argue the part about being "highfalutin," as Theo had said, though I preferred the term classy. Mori was short for Countess Moreau, and she dressed like royalty. On this night, she was wearing a shimmery dark-gold gown that contrasted beautifully with her dark skin. Her black hair was coiled on top of her head, and the shape made me think of a crown.

Felipe ran up to Mori and jumped onto the bench next to her. She idly scratched the spot between his ears as she turned to me. "I know you're not a fan of the *Nightmare Journal* building," she began.

"Why, just because I chased a shape-shifting killer through there?" I asked wryly.

"Exactly. But you should go there and look through past issues. Specifically, take a look at letters to the editor. And you should tell your policeman friend to do the same."

"Why?" I could tell Mori was enjoying keeping me in suspense as she gazed at me with her burnt-orange eyes.

"Because that guy Pete had a lot of letters published. You can build an entire suspect list by noting all the people and businesses he complained about in the newspaper."

CHAPTER FIVE

"First of all," I said, holding up a finger, "what makes you think I'm investigating this murder?"

Mori tilted her head and raised one eyebrow. "I know you."

"And second"—I held up another finger—"why would the newspaper editor publish so many of Pete's letters if they were all hateful?"

Mori gave a little shrug. "That I don't know. I just remember seeing the name Pete Bennett at the bottom of a lot of letters to the editor. He's been writing in to the newspaper for years."

"It sounds like he was known around town for complaining about everything. Even the librarian who found his body said he never had a good word for her."

"One summer, The Caffeinated Cadaver had an iced coffee called the Absent Pete. It was to celebrate him being gone for the summer."

Wow. Even the local coffee shop had disliked him.

"Maybe I should go chat with the baristas there to find out if one of them killed Pete," I said.

"I wouldn't go that far," Mori cautioned. "But after you peruse those letters to the editor, you might want to swing by for some coffee and gossip."

"My kind of investigating."

Justine was just stepping up to the podium at one end of the dining room, and we all fell silent as she began making announcements. I was assigned to the front door, taking tickets, and I was surprised when Justine added, "Also, Olivia, it will be your job to light the jack-o'-lanterns before we open for the night."

I blinked. *What jack-o'-lanterns?*

As soon as the family meeting wrapped up, I made my way to the front of the room and asked Justine just that. She gave me a confused look. "The ones out front," she said.

"When we came back from the library," I responded, "there were no jack-o'-lanterns."

"You haven't been out front since then, have you?" Justine grinned at me. "You'll see them when you get out there. There's been a team working on the display out front. A little something extra for Halloween."

Justine told me I'd find a box of fireplace matches in one of the kitchen drawers, and as soon as I had them in my hand, I headed for the front doors. I had expected to find a small collection of pumpkins, all carved and ready to greet guests with both silly and sinister grins. Instead, I discovered the haunt had spilled out of the vignettes indoors and onto the front lawn.

The Sanctuary had a circular drive in front of it, but it was overgrown, as was the wild area the drive surrounded. At one time, I expected, the wild area had been a carefully manicured garden. There were still flowers and shrubs that weren't native to Arizona growing up amid the dead grass and lifeless stalks.

At the very center of the former garden, where a wooden sign had the name of the haunt painted in what was supposed to look like dripping blood, there was a massive bonfire blazing. Mannequins dressed in black hooded robes stood in a circle around the bonfire, their arms all raised as if they were performing some kind of spell or ritual. Speakers had been cleverly hidden among the dead plants, and creepy orchestral music gave the scene an especially sinister feel.

I found the jack-o'-lanterns lined up along the walkway that led from the parking area to the front entrance. I had expected a dozen. Instead, there must have been at least fifty of them.

The team responsible for the outside decor had been busy.

I passed a lot of people walking up to the ticket window on my way down the path. I had decided to start on the end nearest the parking lot, and by the time I had finally lit the candles inside every pumpkin, it was only three minutes until opening time.

I propped open one of the front doors and began waving people into the entryway, where stanchions and red velvet ropes were set up for the inside queue. There must have been a couple hundred people gathered around the Sanctuary's entrance. Half of them were in line to purchase a ticket, and the other half were lined up in front of the door.

I tore tickets as fast as I could, throwing the stubs into a bin behind the door and giving the remainder back to each guest. By the time the first group had made the back-and-forth trip through the velvet ropes, someone was just opening the door into the haunt itself.

Perfect timing.

I had expected my night to calm down after that initial rush of people, but it never happened. Even though it was only a Thursday, which was typically steady but not outrageously busy, we were absolutely swamped. Malcolm was working the ticket window, taking over for Zach—who couldn't exactly swipe credit cards while in wolf form—

and he didn't shut down sales until exactly one o'clock in the morning.

Apparently, we were all going to work a bit of overtime. I was okay with that, since I was actually having fun. The night had sped by, and people were really in the Halloween spirit, which made chatting with guests easy and enjoyable. A little extra time doing that wouldn't be a problem.

Working late, though, meant I wasn't up and moving the next day until nearly noon. I ate a late breakfast, even though it was technically lunchtime, then walked to the office of *The Nightmare Journal*. The newspaper had been around since Nightmare's mining boom days in the late eighteen hundreds, and the current office was in a building right across the street from the original, much smaller one.

I had to give myself a little pep talk on the fifteen-minute walk, since Mori had been absolutely right about me not wanting to go back into the place. Looking a killer in the face, then chasing them out of the building, could do that to a person.

Luckily, when I walked through the door and up to the reception desk, there were only a few people sitting at desks, and none of them looked murderous. I told the man behind the reception desk I was there to browse through the archives, and he barely looked up from his cell phone screen as he told me to head on down to the basement.

I wasn't sure what year I should begin with, but I did know Pete was a snowbird, which meant he wintered in Nightmare, where the weather was much nicer than it was wherever he lived the rest of the year. I figured Pete must have arrived in town each year by the end of fall, so I selected a bin containing issues from the previous November.

I didn't have to search through many issues before I found the first letter to the editor from Pete.

The issue in my hands was from the Tuesday before Thanksgiving, and Pete had written to complain that the local supermarket didn't have enough turkeys that were small enough to fit into the compact oven inside his RV. It seemed like a really petty thing to complain about, and I was a bit surprised the editor had published it.

I continued my search, and before long, I had found five scathing letters to the editor, all within a three-month period. One of them was from earlier in the year, in February, when Pete had gone on a rant about how the manager of the RV park he lived in was an unethical, unfair man who was only interested in getting more money from his residents.

The most recent letter to the editor was from mid-May. That would have been about the time the temperature was creeping upward with the approach of summer, so it would have made sense that the letters stopped because Pete had gone north.

It also made sense that the letters had stopped because Pete had been murdered.

I briefly considered looking through newspapers from other winters, but there didn't seem to be any point. Mori had been correct that Pete had written a lot of bad things about a lot of people and businesses around Nightmare, and if I tried to compile a suspect list from his letters, it would be an awfully long list.

"Can I help you find something?" a friendly voice called as I was replacing the bin of May issues on the shelf.

I turned to see a slightly disheveled older man smiling at me affably, his blue eyes brilliant, even in the fluorescent overhead lights.

"Oh, I, uh…" I hesitated, then said with a shrug, "I heard Pete Bennett had written a lot of letters to the editor before he was killed. I thought it might be interesting to see what he had to say."

The man laughed heartily enough that a strand of his gray hair slipped down in front of his eyes. As he brushed it back with a hand, he said, "Interesting, hmm? I know who you are, so I'm not surprised you're in the middle of the investigation. I'll warn you, though, that if you look too deeply into those letters, you'll think *I'm* a murder suspect."

"Why?"

"Because I'm Wallace Trim, the editor all those letters were addressed to. Pete had a lot of ire, and I wasn't spared from it."

I nodded. "Is that why you published some pretty silly complaints from him? To appease him?"

"That's exactly why I did it," Wallace said. He sighed and leaned back against the wall. "Pete would hand-deliver those letters to me. I tried to set some boundaries, but he always talked his way past the rest of the staff and made it to my office. Honestly, everyone here was afraid of him because he'd start yelling if he didn't get his way. If I published one of his letters every three or four weeks, Pete would mostly leave me alone."

"And if you didn't?"

"He'd show up where I was having dinner or hound me when I was at the saloon with friends. Once, he accosted me at the barber shop. Believe me, I understand why the police might want to bring me in for questioning."

"It sounds like it was awful for you, but I don't think you had motive for murder."

"Someone beheaded a seventy-three-year-old man whose worst offense was crankiness," Wallace said. "I don't think the killer had a good motive. I think they were just sick and tired of Pete threatening to run everyone in Nightmare out of business."

"By that calculation," I said, "half the town must be on the suspect list."

"The police have their work cut out for them," Wallace

agreed with a nod. "I know I teased you about your interest in this case, but they can use all the help they can get. And, if you ever decide you want to pursue investigative journalism, you let me know. I'm always on the lookout for good freelancers."

I shouldn't have been surprised that Wallace knew about the murders I had solved. After all, this was Nightmare, where everyone seemed to know everyone else's business, and it was the newspaper's job to help with that. But to know the newspaper editor was keeping tabs on me—and would even give me some work, if I wanted it—made me feel rather proud of myself.

I walked out of the newspaper office with my head held high, and I smiled as I walked down High Noon Boulevard toward home. The street was the hub of tourist activity, since it had been made to look like the Wild West town Nightmare had once been. The paved street had been topped with dirt, and the Western-style buildings on either side of it were fronted by covered boardwalks.

The stores and restaurants had gone all out for Halloween, and virtually every display window I passed had a skeletal cowboy posed among plastic jack-o'-lanterns and foam headstones.

When I passed by the saloon, I heard eerie music pouring out from the doorway, which had two short swinging doors. The inside was just as "old-timey saloon" as the entrance.

Above the music, I heard a long, high wail.

I began to laugh at the silly Halloween sound effects, until I realized the wail had come from a real person, just like Renee's scream at the library.

An older woman was standing in front of the saloon, her face twisted in a mix of anger and grief. She pressed the tip of her index finger against the chest of the bearded man who stood opposite her.

I realized the man was the doctor I had seen checking out a book about malpractice law at the library.

As I watched, the woman opened her mouth again. Instead of wailing this time, though, she began to yell.

"You did it! You killed my husband!"

CHAPTER SIX

"Maris!" the doctor hissed. He looked around quickly to see if anyone was listening in on the conversation, and I hastily averted my eyes and tried to look like a casual passerby.

I'm pretty sure I completely failed.

"You can't deny it, Doc!" Maris yelled. "You killed Pete to avoid the malpractice suit!" Her long dark hair was shot with silver, and it was pulled back in a low ponytail. Strands of hair had come loose, though, giving her a slightly wild look. She was easily a foot shorter than the doctor, but she looked like she might pounce on him at any moment.

"I did no such thing," Doc retorted. "You think he's the first patient who's ever threatened a malpractice suit? It happens in my line of work. I've never killed anyone for it."

Maris was shaking her head, the loose strands of hair flying around her narrow face. "You got to him before he could head north for the summer!"

Doc's face had been steadily growing red, and his eyebrows drew down as he glared at Maris.

The argument was drawing a crowd, and someone stepped between them. I couldn't hear what the man said, but Doc seemed to deflate a little.

Maris, on the other hand, gave the man a stern look. "Not now, Aaron. I can handle myself!"

I stepped up to Maris. "I'm going to the police station," I said. Actually, I wasn't. I had been planning to call Reyes about the letters to the editor once I got home, but the police station wasn't far from the saloon, and it seemed like a good way to get Maris away from the confrontation. "Why don't you come with me? You can report your suspicion to Officer Reyes."

Maris looked from me to Doc several times, then nodded curtly. "Fine." She stabbed a finger toward him again. "This isn't over!"

Before she was finished, Maris turned to the man who had stepped between her and Doc. "And don't you lecture me about making a scene!"

The man—Aaron, Maris had called him—looked like he wanted to retort, but he wisely kept his mouth shut.

The watching crowd parted as Maris stalked away from Doc and Aaron, the boardwalk echoing with the sound of her angry stomping. Once I had caught up to her, I said, "I'm sorry about your husband. Do you really think he was killed back in the spring?"

"The police said so." Maris was still wound up, and her tone seemed to be daring me to disagree with her. "They told me his condition indicated he'd been in that basement for about six months."

No wonder he smelled bad.

"Did you think he was just missing?" I asked. "Or were you searching for him back in your hometown?"

Maris shook her head. "I thought he'd gone back to our house in Ohio. I stayed here all summer."

"And you weren't worried when you never heard from him?"

The last of the anger seemed to drain from Maris. Her shoulders rolled forward, and her chin drooped. "We were separated. About a year ago. I got my own RV to live in here in Nightmare, and Pete kept living in the one we used to share. One day in May, his RV wasn't there anymore, and I figured he'd gone back to Ohio for the summer."

"The killer timed it perfectly to make it look like Pete had simply left town," I mused. They had even driven off in Pete's RV to complete the charade.

"I thought it was typical of him to leave and not tell me," Maris said. "Of course, as it turns out, he was dead." Maris paused. We were halfway to the police station by then, and her footsteps slowed. "I know I'm a suspect, but I didn't kill him."

"I'm sure you've been as helpful as possible in this investigation," I soothed. "The police will find the real killer."

When we reached the police station, Maris and I walked into the reception area at the same time as Reyes, who was just coming out of the hallway that led to the back of the station. He stopped and put his hands on his hips. "Here with another tip, Olivia?"

"Actually, Maris here wanted to give you a tip," I said.

"Is this about your shouting match with Doc just now?" Reyes asked, raising an eyebrow at Maris.

"The gossip traveled faster than me," Maris said flatly. "Yes. I think he killed my husband."

"You can fill me in once we get to my office." Reyes turned his glance to me. "And, somehow, you wound up in the middle of things again."

"I was just heading home from the newspaper office."

Reyes bit his lip, and his expression was somewhere between wanting to laugh at me and wanting to lecture me. "I've already had a chat with Wallace about Pete's letters to him," he said. "But I appreciate you double-checking my work."

I opened my mouth to respond, but Reyes held up a

hand to stop me. "And, yes, we know Pete was practically stalking Wallace."

"Who cares about the newspaper editor?" Maris said, her eyes narrowed at Reyes. "Doc did it!"

Reyes stepped to the side and waved Maris in the direction of his office. "You didn't mention this theory when we spoke yesterday," he said. "Come on. You can fill me in."

Maris headed down the hallway without a second glance at me, but Reyes paused long enough to give me a searching look. Sometimes, I was certain, Reyes suspected I was somehow behind all the murders in this town.

It wasn't my fault dead bodies kept falling into my life.

A few minutes later, I was on High Noon Boulevard again. This time, I barely noticed all the Halloween decor along the way. I was too busy thinking about Maris and Doc and all the many other suspects in this murder case.

When I drew level with the saloon again, I heard more shouting. This time, it was between two men, and I quickly realized no one was actually having an argument. Not a real one, at any rate.

Instead, it was two costumed actors portraying the outlaw Butch Tanner and former Nightmare sheriff Connor McCrory. The two men had killed each other in a shootout on that very street, back in the eighteen hundreds. Every day, there were three reenactments of the duel, and the tourists absolutely ate it up.

The boardwalk was crowded with people gathering to watch the show, so instead of trying to worm my way past them, I stopped to take in the entertainment, too. I had to laugh when I saw both actors had added Halloween elements to their costumes. McCrory's black hat and long duster had been covered with fake cobwebs. The real Butch Tanner had worn a red bandana over his mouth and nose, but the actor playing him had chosen an orange one that had a black jack-o'-lantern face on it.

The two actors had just moved into position in the middle of the street, kicking up dust with their spurred boots, when a gruesome, rotten face suddenly popped up in front of me. I shrieked and jumped backward, drawing laughter from the people nearby.

The man who had scared me straightened up, his zombie makeup making his own laughter downright creepy. "Happy Halloween!" he said in a raspy voice before loping off down the boardwalk.

I was still gazing after the zombie when I heard the pop of the guns. The blanks in the six-shooters the Tanner and McCrory reenactors used were harmless but loud.

A zombie and a Wild West shootout. This town is so strange.

And yet, for some reason, I absolutely loved it.

My mood had been dampened by the confrontation between Maris and Doc, but after watching the reenactment, I felt a lot better. The real Tanner and McCrory were still around, albeit as ghosts who haunted the Sanctuary, and I liked being one of the people who could say they actually knew the legendary pair.

Of course, I couldn't say that to many people, because it would get me a lot of bizarre looks.

When I reached Cowboy's Corral Motor Lodge, I decided to pop into the front office before heading to my efficiency apartment at the back of the property. When I went inside, Mama Dalton was sitting on the floor while her granddaughter, Lucy, stood rigidly in front of her. Mama was making adjustments to the hemline of Lucy's pink satin dress.

Lucy looked like a princess, albeit one with wild hair. Her dark curls seemed especially rebellious that day.

Lucy's eyes slid in my direction, then lit up with joy. Her lips compressed, like she wanted to smile but was trying so hard to stand still that even that small motion would be unacceptable.

Mama had turned her head in my direction when I walked into the office, and her face broke into a grin. "We're making progress!" she said, gesturing toward the dress. "Lucy, honey, you can relax for a minute. I want to talk to Olivia."

Lucy walked over to me, stopped about a foot away, and leaned in to give me a hug around the waist with just her hands and forearms. "Sorry, Miss Olivia, but if I get closer, I'll wrinkle my Halloween costume!"

"That's okay, Lucy. I can't wait to see the whole costume tomorrow!"

"I meant to get it finished sooner, but we've just been so busy," Mama said. She slowly got up from the floor. "Oh, I'm getting too old for this. Anyway, I brought my sewing machine so I can work on the costume in between helping guests."

Mama and her husband, Benny, owned Cowboy's Corral, and her family had been the first to make me feel welcome in Nightmare. I had been on my way to San Diego when my hunk-of-junk car had broken down just outside the old mining town, and it had been Mama's son —Lucy's dad—who had towed my car and dropped me off at the motel that wound up becoming my home.

Mama stretched, then reached up to smooth her fluffy white hair. "I hear you were just at the police station," she said casually.

Again, I was reminded of just how quickly Nightmare gossip spread.

I made a show of looking behind me. "Is someone following me and reporting everything I do back to you?"

"My friend Jody saw you coming out of the police station, but she didn't call me to report that. She was calling to say that right after you left, a police car pulled up, and someone was taken into the station in handcuffs."

42

Mama seemed to revel in holding me in suspense, and I made a go-ahead motion with my hand. "Who was it? And for what?"

"Renee Porter, the librarian who found Pete's body, was just arrested for his murder!"

CHAPTER SEVEN

"No. No way," I said, shaking my head. I had made Mama repeat the news twice because I just couldn't believe my ears. "That makes no sense."

"Nevertheless, they seemed to think she had motive," Mama said, shrugging. "I've known Renee for years, and I wouldn't have pegged her as a murderer, either."

"I had a chat with Wallace Trim, the newspaper editor, earlier," I said thoughtfully. "He speculated that Pete wasn't killed for anything really significant. Wallace thinks someone just got tired of him complaining all the time and finally snapped."

"And I know for a fact Pete was mean to Renee." Mama nodded knowingly. "I even saw him berating her once while I was waiting to check out a book. However, my friend Jody suggested Renee might have had a better motive than just being sick and tired of Pete's behavior."

"Oh?" Out of the corner of my eye, I saw Lucy twirling in circles, the bottom of her dress fanning out. She seemed oblivious to our conversation, which was good. She was only ten, so I didn't want to fill her head with thoughts of murder.

"Pete had been trying to get the library shut down," Mama continued. "It was like his own personal crusade last winter. He went all over town saying the wiring in the

45

library wasn't up to code, and he knew because he had been an electrician before he retired. Pete went to the mayor's office, demanding the library be closed, and when that didn't get him anywhere, he began going to every city council meeting to voice his displeasure."

"Was he right, though? About the wiring?"

Mama gave a little snort. "Half the buildings in this town have old wiring because they're old buildings. As long as the systems are functioning safely, there's no need to replace them. The library is no exception, but Pete always had to have something to be angry about."

"Renee's arrest makes more sense, at least," I said. "But that still leaves some very big questions. For one, how did that tiny little lady chop off a man's head, drag the body to the basement, then stash it in a prop coffin?"

"Maybe she lured him down there. She could have asked him to show her the electrical wiring in the basement."

"Or, she could have had an accomplice who stashed the body for her." I suddenly shook my head. "No, I still can't believe Renee is the one responsible. She seems nice. Plus, why in the world would she have stashed the body at her own workplace? Or told us about the body in the first place?"

Mama shrugged. "If she wanted to make herself look innocent, pretending to be shocked by the discovery of the body was a good way to do it."

"True."

"Though you do make a good point about Renee chopping off a head. How would she know how to decapitate someone in the first place?" Mama gave herself a shake. "Yuck. So messy."

I began to laugh. "Actually, I bet it would have been easy for her to learn the best way to decapitate a body! She's a librarian. Look at the wealth of information she has at her fingertips. A book on anatomy might do the trick."

Mama's blue eyes grew wide. "Librarians might be the most dangerous people of all."

"But I love the library!" Lucy piped up. She had stopped twirling and was staring at us. "Mrs. Lopez is the librarian at my school, and she's the best."

"Of course she is!" Mama said quickly. "Olivia and I were only joking."

"We were just agreeing that librarians are great at finding any information they need," I added.

Though, for that matter, the same information available to Renee was available to anyone who walked into that library.

"Speaking of school, Lucy," I said, glancing at my watch. "Shouldn't you be there right now?"

Lucy made a *tsk* noise and planted her hands on her hips. "Halloween in Nightmare is kind of a big deal, you know. We only have a half day on Halloween, except this year, Halloween is on a Saturday, so we got our half day today."

"The school transforms the gym into a little haunt every year," Mama said. "It's a fundraiser for the after-school activities. Lots of the kids and parents are spending the afternoon there, helping set it up."

"Oh, how fun. Looks like Nightmare Sanctuary is going to have some competition this weekend."

"Actually," Mama said, giving me a sly look, "you should take Lucy over there to do a little volunteer work. They'll be happy to have you since you work at a real haunted attraction, and Lucy will have fun decorating with her friends. I'll stay here and hem her dress."

"Judging by your expression, this is about more than me doing my civic duty."

"You'll hear lots of gossip if you go," Mama said,

nodding. "And my guess is the murder will be the hot topic."

I had been planning to spend my Friday afternoon getting some marketing work done for the motel. When I had broken down in Nightmare, I had been fresh off a divorce and a bankruptcy filing. Mama had taken pity on me, offering me the efficiency apartment in exchange for doing marketing for Cowboy's Corral. I had done marketing when I lived in Nashville, and my work at the Sanctuary left me free to do things for the motel during the day. It was the perfect setup for me.

Instead of marketing work, though, it looked like I would be doing some sleuthing.

Lucy loved the idea of helping set up the school's haunt, so she changed back into her jeans and pink T-shirt, and we were soon on our way to Nightmare Elementary School.

The gym's transformation was well underway when Lucy and I walked inside. There were stacks of cardboard boxes arranged to form a narrow, winding trail across the basketball court. They had been painted black, and volunteers were busy adding details, like dripping red letters that read, *Turn Back!* and old, slightly creepy photographs that had probably been flea market finds.

On the far side of the gym, there was a check-in table. Lucy and I headed there and were assigned to help decorate one section of the path. Soon, I was armed with a bag of fake cobwebs and a roll of tape. Lucy had white and red paint pens clutched in her hand, and her job was to draw creepy things on the cardboard boxes.

The volunteers around us were doing the same sorts of things, and everyone was chatting happily as they painted or hung photos.

"Seems weird to be setting up a haunted house right after the murder," one woman said.

A man nearby laughed. "I feel sorry for the volunteers assigned to the crypt scene! Imagine how they feel looking into those fake coffins!"

"It's true, then?" someone else chimed in. "The body was really in a fake coffin?"

"It really was," the man said. "The rumor is that the librarian did it!"

There was a chorus of "Ooh!" from the people around me.

"Did you ever read the victim's letters to the editor?" I asked. "I chatted with Wallace Trim this morning, and it sounds like he felt he was being personally attacked by all of Pete's letters."

The woman who had brought up the murder laughed loudly. "That's because he was personally attacked! Quite literally. Pete jumped him at the saloon one night."

CHAPTER EIGHT

"A seventy-three-year-old man jumped someone?" I asked. "Pete must have been awfully spry."

"Oh, yeah, he was," the man said. "I'm pretty sure his ire is what kept him alive and kicking."

"Plus," a man farther down the cardboard path called out, "Pete was drunk when he attacked Wallace. I'm sure that helped fuel his aggression."

Wallace had made Pete's behavior sound bad, especially when he told me about Pete following him to places like the barber shop, but it was a lot worse knowing Pete had physically attacked him. What else hadn't Wallace shared with me? And, had he called himself out as a suspect as a trick, so I wouldn't think he *was* a suspect?

Maybe that offer to write for the newspaper had been a way to throw me off the scent, I realized.

The first man's chest puffed out proudly, and he turned toward me with a plastic monster mask clutched in his hands. "I was there that night," he said. "At the saloon. Saw the whole thing. Aaron had to jump in to break it up, though he didn't seem to know whose side he was on. Sure, Pete lived at his RV park, but that meant he was right there to make Aaron's life even more miserable."

"And Aaron would have been mad at Wallace for publishing that letter about him," the woman who had first brought up the topic of the murder said. "Aaron comes into the Nightmare Credit Union all the time, and he was furious for weeks after it was published."

The name Aaron was familiar to me, and as I continued taping long strands of cobwebs to the top edges of the cardboard trail, I realized why. When Maris and Doc had gotten into their shouting match outside the saloon, she had called the man who jumped in to break it up Aaron.

He seemed to always be on hand to break up fights. Did the guy manage an RV park, or was he the bouncer at Nightmare Saloon?

I was making a mental note to stop by the RV park for a chat with Aaron when I felt small fingers against my own. I looked down to see Lucy, who had managed to get a streak of red paint on her cheek.

Lucy squeezed my hand. "Miss Olivia, I'm trying to finish the scary face I drew, but I can't reach high enough to make the hair. Can you please come help?"

"Of course! Lead the way!"

Lucy deftly weaved through the volunteers working in our section of the haunt, while I bumped my way through, muttering, "Excuse me. Sorry. Excuse me."

We turned a corner in the path, and I had just registered that we had walked into a wider area when someone popped out from behind a white sheet, which had been spattered with red paint to look like blood.

I screamed for the second time that day, and this person wasn't even in a costume. It was just a teenager, whom I figured was somebody's big brother, there to help build the haunt.

Lucy was nearly doubled over with laughter. "Oh, I got you!"

"You set this up," I said, pursing my lips at her and trying my best to glare. I failed completely, because in truth, I was quite proud of her. Lucy had been allowed to spend a few hours inside Nightmare Sanctuary Haunted House with me just a week before, and she had loved playing a creepy pirate and scaring the guests who came through. The kid had a knack for fright.

The teenage boy was laughing, too, but he stopped abruptly and said, "Watch this!" He clutched at his throat and made choking noises, his eyes rolling up in his head and his tongue sticking out. He staggered backward while glancing surreptitiously over his shoulder to see where he was going.

When the boy reached a plywood coffin lying on hay bales along one side of the scene, he pitched backward into it, coming to a rest with his hands crossed over his chest and his eyes closed.

Lucy squealed with delight and clapped her hands. I, however, gasped. Mama and I had doubted Renee would have been able to get Pete's body into the coffin, since he had been so much bigger than her. Seeing the teen made me realize that just a little precise tipping would have levered Pete right into the coffin.

That meant Renee really could have murdered Pete. For that matter, Maris could have done it, too.

Of course, that would have meant Pete was beheaded after he had been tipped into the coffin. Maybe the police would discover he had been killed a different way, like with poison, and the beheading was done afterward to hide his identity.

Another thing I wondered was whether I would be able to pry those details out of Officer Reyes.

Lucy and I were soon back at work on the haunt, but my mind was, for better or for worse, focused more on anatomy than on the cobwebs I was hanging. After beheading Pete, why not keep chopping him up? Renee was too petite to haul a body up the library's basement steps, but she could have taken him out a piece at a time. It was a disgusting way to remove evidence, but it would have worked.

Again, I was curious to know what the killer had been thinking by leaving the body where it would eventually be found. Was the killer sloppy or overly confident, or was there some other answer to the question?

I had to be at work by seven o'clock, but I was determined to meet Aaron first. Lucy and I wrapped up at the school around five o'clock, when the finishing touches were being put on the haunt.

As we walked outside into the late-afternoon sun, Lucy was bouncing with every step. "Tomorrow, on Halloween, I get to come to the haunt here, and then Mom and Dad are going to take me to the one at the library, and then we're going to go see you, and Mister Damien, and all my other friends at the Sanctuary!"

I smiled at Lucy's love for Halloween and haunted houses. "I promise I'll save the best candy for you," I told her. The Sanctuary would open a few hours early on Halloween, but instead of scaring adults, we would be handing out candy to kids. Justine had told me it was an annual tradition at the Sanctuary.

"You have cobwebs in your hair," Lucy said offhandedly as we climbed into my car.

Well, at least they aren't real cobwebs. I ran my fingers through my shoulder-length auburn hair, pulling out long white strands. I was grateful for Lucy pointing them out, because I didn't want to walk into the RV park's office looking like some kind of haunted house castoff.

I realized as we drove back to Cowboy's Corral that I had no idea where the RV park Pete had lived at was located. For that matter, I didn't know its name.

But I knew who would know. I parked right in front of the motel office, under the covered area reserved for people checking into the motel, and walked inside with Lucy. I had to wait a good ten minutes for Lucy to finish giving Mama a blow-by-blow account of our time at the school before I could ask about the RV park.

"Nightmare Holiday Park," Mama said without hesitation. "Yes, Pete had enough of a reputation in this town that everyone knew where he lived. It's off the main road, south of town. You can't miss it."

I thanked Mama for the information and headed out. I quickly passed by what was considered Nightmare's downtown area and began keeping my eyes peeled for Nightmare Holiday Park.

I shouldn't have been worried about missing the place. Mama had been right: there was no way I would have overlooked the massive neon sign out front. *Nightmare* was in red capital letters, giving the sign a bit of a sinister look. It was appropriate for Halloween, but perhaps not for a place people lived year-round.

The road through the RV park seemed to be a long oval, and it was one-way. A faded wooden sign said the office was straight ahead, so I drove slowly and took in the neighborhood.

Half of the parking pads were empty, and I figured a lot of the snowbirds still hadn't arrived for winter in the desert. The RVs I passed ranged from the super-fancy kind, which probably cost just as much as a house, to more humble ones that had some wear and tear.

The office was at the very back of the property, inside a small adobe building underneath a sprawling mesquite tree. There were no parking spaces, so I pulled as far to one side of the road as I could and hoped anyone trying to drive past would have enough room.

It was only as I was opening the red door that led into the office that I glanced to my right and saw there was, in fact, a parking area. It was so screened by some low bushes I hadn't seen it from the road.

And, to my dismay, there was a police car parked there. I could already picture the exasperation on Reyes's face if I walked into the office and came face-to-face with him.

Please don't be Reyes, I repeated to myself as I continued on into the office.

It was. He was sitting at one of two threadbare gray chairs in front of a wide desk. Behind the desk sat the man whom I had seen break up the argument between Maris and Doc.

Reyes and Aaron were so focused on each other that neither one seemed to register my presence at first. As I stood there, considering whether I should just back right out the door and leave, Aaron dropped a thick stack of papers onto the desk.

"Here are all of his unpaid fees," Aaron said, a note of bitterness in his tone. "But I didn't kill him over it."

CHAPTER NINE

Aaron's eyes turned to me as he sat back in his chair.

"No one is accusing you of murder," Reyes said evenly. He finally seemed to realize Aaron's attention had shifted away from him, and he turned to follow his gaze. When Reyes saw it was me at the door, he shook his head. "I should have known."

"Can I help you?" Aaron asked me.

I looked at Aaron, then at Reyes, then back at Aaron. Talk about awkward. I tried to think of an excuse for being there, but my brain couldn't formulate anything plausible under that kind of pressure. Instead, I stood silently, shifting my weight from one foot to the other.

To my surprise, it was Aaron who broke the silence. "Wait a minute," he said slowly. "I've seen you before, and not just outside the saloon earlier. You were at the Fall Festival a couple weeks ago. You were with the Shackleford kid."

"He's in his forties, like me," I pointed out.

Aaron shrugged. "He'll always be Baxter's kid to me. One of those Sanctuary freaks."

I bristled at the term. The vast majority of the people in Nightmare had no idea the supernatural world existed, which meant they thought the people living and working at the Sanctuary were just normal humans.

Except, some Nightmare residents didn't think we were normal. They thought we were freaks.

I was surprised for the second time in only a minute when Reyes slid to the edge of his seat and said in a warning tone, "They're good people over at the Sanctuary. Just because they keep to themselves doesn't make them strange."

Reyes and I were sometimes at odds—which I wholly admitted was my fault, since I was the one always barging my way into murder investigations—but in that moment, I wanted to hug him.

Aaron's shoulders hitched upward, and I imagined he was trying his best not to roll his eyes. "Anything else, officer?" he asked pointedly.

"Yes," Reyes said, all business again. "On what exact date did you notice Pete's RV was gone?"

"Oh, it was one night in early May."

"An exact date, please," Reyes reminded him.

With a sigh that implied he was the most put-upon man on the planet, Aaron pulled out a spiral-bound planner. He flipped through the pages slowly, glancing up at Reyes now and then.

If he's trying to be annoying, then it's working, I thought. I could only see one side of Reyes's face, since he was facing Aaron, but I could see enough to know Reyes was losing his patience.

"It was the same day I got the bill for all the plumbing work I had to get done to this place," Aaron said, making a show of turning more pages. "I remember that well, because I'll be paying off that and the electrical work until someone murders *me*. Ah, here. May the fifth. I woke up that morning and was making my usual rounds in the golf cart, and I saw Pete's parking pad was empty. He snuck out in the middle of the night so he wouldn't ever have to pay all the back rent he owed me."

"Did you ask Maris to help you get the money you were owed?" I asked.

Aaron narrowed his faded gray eyes at me, the corners of his mouth turning down. Even though he was looking at me, he addressed Reyes. "What's her deal? Does she work for you at the police department?"

"She's asking a valid question," Reyes pointed out. "Mrs. Bennett could have helped you get the money since they shared a bank account."

"No, they didn't," Aaron said. "After Maris and Pete separated, Maris opened her own bank account. She always paid me on time. To her credit, she tried talking some sense into him, but Pete wasn't having any of it. No surprise there."

"Hmm." Reyes snapped his notebook shut. "I'll follow up with Mrs. Bennett. Thank you for your time."

Aaron mumbled something that didn't sound at all like *you're welcome.*

I was out the door before Reyes had even stood up, but he quickly caught up with me.

"Olivia," he said.

I turned, wincing at the way he had said my name. There was a lecture coming. I could feel it.

Reyes crossed his arms. "If you had learned anything from Aaron, would you have passed it on to me?"

"Absolutely," I assured him.

"Then, next time, just call me and tell me when you're itching to talk to a suspect. I'll do it for you, so you don't have to be the middle man." Reyes paused, and his stern expression relaxed. "And, if you're lucky, I'll let you come with me."

Not the lecture I had been expecting. I sighed and felt my shoulders relax. "Thanks. And sorry."

"Try to stay out of trouble tonight, okay? And out of my investigation."

"I'll be at work, so no trouble, and no investigating!" I gave Reyes a tentative smile.

Reyes smiled back. "Good."

I kept my word, going straight back to my apartment from the RV park so I could eat a quick dinner and put on my black Nightmare Sanctuary T-shirt. My orange shag rug was as close as my little efficiency apartment had to Halloween decor, and I promised myself that I'd carve a jack-o'-lantern next year. At least I'd get to see all the ones at the Sanctuary when I arrived for work that night.

The weather had cooled off a lot since the extreme heat of late summer, and although it wasn't the chilly October weather I had been used to in Nashville, the night still had a nice cool feel. I decided to walk to work. It was about a mile, but I had the time, and I wanted to enjoy the light breeze.

There was a steady stream of cars along the two-lane road that led toward the Sanctuary, so I had to walk carefully, but soon, I was turning right at the old gallows and onto the lane to the Sanctuary.

The narrow dirt lane had a crest in it, and it wasn't until reaching its peak that the former hospital building could be seen below. The weathered gray stone and unforgiving architecture was absolutely perfect for a haunted house, and I knew it would look even better with the bonfire scene out front. By walking, I would be able to stop and appreciate the view in a way I just couldn't if I had driven.

The scene that met my eyes when I reached the top of the hill was every bit as spooky and dramatic as I had hoped it would be. I stood as far off the road as I could without bumping into a cactus or some other sharp desert plant and soaked in the view for a couple of minutes. Then, it was time to head inside.

I had just enough time to catch up with Damien before

that night's family meeting. He was sitting at the wide oak desk in his office, staring at the screen of his laptop. Since the door was open, I just knocked lightly on the doorframe as I walked in, and he looked up and smiled.

Then, his smile faded just as quickly. "Something is on your mind," he prompted. "I can see it on your face."

I dropped into one of the oxblood leather chairs in front of the desk. I didn't want to repeat Aaron's words verbatim, but his comment about Sanctuary people was weighing on me, so I shrugged. "This community's attitude toward those of us who work at the Sanctuary is a little... discouraging."

"Oh, so you ran into someone who called us freaks?" Damien nodded knowingly.

"Yeah. How did you know it was that exact word?"

Damien waved a hand around. "I grew up here. It was an easy guess." He folded his arms on his desk, and I could see the flash of silver from the cufflinks on his crisp black shirt. "You weren't an outsider in Nashville, were you?"

"Of course not. My marketing work meant I was a big part of the community there." Damien knew that already, of course, but I understood the point he was trying to make. "And if I had come to Nightmare a couple years ago, before my life fell apart, I probably would have been just as judgmental about the people here."

"Good thing you didn't come here a couple years ago," Damien said. He smiled softly. "There are a lot of good people in Nightmare, Olivia. The ones who call us names and judge us are just the most vocal, and I assure you, they don't speak for the whole town."

"I know, but thank you for the reminder."

"There are plenty of rude people in this town, though," I heard Zach say behind me.

I twisted around in my chair to find him standing in the

doorway, his long, rust-red hair pulled back in a ponytail and his faded jeans looking extra tight on his muscular legs.

"You're human again," I commented. "Welcome back."

"Sure," Zach intoned. He was usually grumpy but never more so than right after transitioning from his wolf form back to his human form. He much preferred being a wolf.

"Don't you have something to say to me?" I prompted.

"I do, actually. How did you know I was coming here to talk to you instead of Damien?"

"Because I'm the one you nearly sent flying yesterday."

Zach looked confused for a moment, then he said, "Ah. Right. You're expecting me to apologize for smacking into you when I was coming out of the dining room. I actually went there first to look for you tonight, because I meant what I just said about rude people. Some old guy just pushed his way to the front of the line and demanded to see 'the nosy lady.' I can only assume he meant you."

"Who is he?" I asked.

"No idea. He's in the entryway, waiting for you." Zach jerked his head in that direction.

Damien stood at the same time I did, clearly not willing to let me go talk to the stranger alone. I didn't argue.

I also didn't point out to Zach that he had yet to apologize to me. I could remind him later.

When I emerged from the hallway into the entryway, where the red velvet ropes were waiting to welcome the horde of guests already lined up outside, I saw a familiar man standing there. Really, it wasn't the face I recognized immediately, but the bushy white beard.

"You're the doctor," I said in greeting.

"Donald Fitz," the man said. "But everyone calls me Doc."

"I understand you wanted to see me?" *You know*, I thought sarcastically, *me, the nosy one.*

Doc took a deep breath. "Yes. I know you help find killers, and I want to hire you to clear my name in Pete Bennett's death."

Was Doc yet another person announcing themself as a suspect in Pete's murder? I had joked about conjuring for easy clues, but this wasn't what I had anticipated.

"The police are on top of it," I said. "If you're being honest with them, then you don't have anything to worry about."

"That's just it," Doc said, his eyes darting around the room nervously. "I'm not being honest with the police."

CHAPTER TEN

"Why aren't you being honest with the police, Doc?" I asked.

Doc was still looking around, and when he spoke again, his voice was low. "Pete was right to threaten a malpractice suit against me. I made a mistake, and as much as I want to delete his medical file and all evidence of it, that would make me look even more guilty of murder."

"And you're afraid that telling the police about it would also make you look guilty?" I guessed.

Doc laughed sardonically. "That would be the least of my worries! If word gets out, I risk losing my license, and my reputation. I'm trusting you not to turn me in. I've been taking care of this town for thirty-five years, and I'm a good doctor."

"I'm sure you are," I said. "Look, I'm not trying to clear anyone's name, but I do want the killer to be found. And if that means me being nosy, then so be it."

Doc, at least, had the grace to look slightly ashamed. "Sorry. I didn't know your name. Just keep up the good work, okay? I'd like to get through this unscathed."

I nodded, even while thinking that Doc was most definitely still on the suspect list. And, when I needed a doctor in the future, I might want to look elsewhere.

Doc left, and I had just enough time to briefly discuss

the surprise visit with Damien and Zach before Zach said, "I have to get back to the ticket window. You wouldn't believe the crowd outside. If it's this bad tonight, what will tomorrow be like?"

"This bad?" Damien repeated, grinning. "I think you mean this good! This is our most lucrative weekend of the year."

"And I've got to get to the family meeting before we start welcoming all those people who are paying good money to get scared." I gave Damien and Zach a little salute and headed in the direction of the dining room.

The first thing Justine said when she stepped up to the podium to begin that night's family meeting was that we would all need to report for duty at three o'clock the following day. "We'll have a quick meeting, then get ready for the kids who will be trick-or-treating through the haunt. Fiona, these are young little ears, so please, no full banshee wails. And Theo, no making kids cry this year!"

"That was an accident! I was only trying to scare them a little bit," Theo protested from his spot on the bench beside me. He leaned his head toward me and whispered, "But it was pretty funny!"

Once again, I was on duty at the front door, taking tickets. I was also tasked with lighting all the jack-o'-lanterns again, and as soon as the meeting wrapped up, I hustled to start that process. I didn't want to cut things so close to opening time again.

This time, I got the door propped open and began tearing tickets with seven minutes to spare. By the time the door to the haunt opened so the first guests could go through, the entryway was full of eager people. I was getting the hang of lighting jack-o'-lanterns.

And then, suddenly, it was one o'clock in the morning, and the last group was entering the haunt. I had been so busy all night, and having so much fun, that the time had absolutely flown by.

I always kept my purse in a locker inside the staff ladies' room, and after I retrieved it, I walked in the direction of the entrance, calling good night to everyone I passed. When Clara sailed by, she gave me a wide grin. "Happy Halloween, Olivia!"

I was about to argue that Halloween wasn't until the next day, but since it was well after midnight, the next day had already arrived. "Happy Halloween, Clara!"

On my walk home, I realized I really was happy. I had loved Halloween as a kid, of course, but once I grew up, the holiday would pass each year without me really noticing. I had been more interested in designer clothes than costumes.

Here at the Sanctuary, though, I couldn't help but be excited about Halloween. Everyone around me loved the holiday, and the Sanctuary was absolutely perfect for it— after all, it felt a bit like Halloween there every night of the year.

I might have been excited, but I was also worn out. Ten minutes after I got back to Cowboy's Corral, I was in bed, asleep. My alarm was set for ten o'clock the next morning, and I don't think I stirred until its beeping ripped me out of a dream about going to a party hosted by ghosts.

After a shower and coffee, I decided to head up to the motel office to chat with Mama. Normally, the bell above the office door would tinkle when anyone came in or out. Since it was Halloween, though, Mama had put a motion-sensor speaker next to the door, so when I walked in, a loud scream sounded through the room.

There was black crepe paper strung across the ceiling, and cardboard Halloween decorations were tacked to the windows and walls. The designs were mostly black cats and smiling jack-o'-lanterns, and they all looked cute and old-fashioned.

"Vintage," Mama said in greeting, as if she knew exactly what I was thinking. "I wanted our Halloween decor to be from the same era the motel was built."

"It's perfect," I said. Cowboy's Corral Motor Lodge had been built decades before, when road trips along winding two-lane highways were all the rage. The neon sign out front, which featured a cowboy taking a snooze, was an icon of a bygone era.

Mama and I got to chatting about the murder case. "Everyone keeps admitting to me that they're a suspect because they had motive," I told her. "If only someone would admit to being the actual killer!"

"I figured you were still hard at work on this case, so I came prepared this morning." Mama reached down behind the Formica check-in counter and pulled out two white pastry boxes. "These are for you."

I laughed. "Solving a murder is hard work, but it doesn't make me *that* hungry!"

"They're not for you to *eat*," Mama clarified. She put the boxes on the counter and slid them in my direction. "One is for Luis Reyes, and the other is for Renee Porter. I figured you'd be visiting her in jail to see if she also names herself as a suspect."

"The police certainly think she is one. And, given Pete's threats to get the library shut down, I can understand why." I thanked Mama for the baked goods, since it gave me a good excuse to visit Renee, but I added, "Why does Reyes get a box, too?"

Mama shrugged. "Because he's a nice guy who puts up with you always being in the middle of his murder investigations. He's earned it."

"That he has," I agreed.

Since I had two boxes of what I soon discovered were

cinnamon rolls—sprinkled with black and orange sugar, no less—I decided to drive to the police station rather than walking. Reyes wasn't there, so I left his box at the reception desk, along with a note wishing him a happy Halloween.

The jail cells at the back of the building weren't meant for holding anyone long-term, and Mama's vintage Halloween decor would have fit right in with the short, old-fashioned row of cells. The iron bars looked like something from an old gangster movie.

Renee was sitting in the last cell, and she had made herself quite at home. There was a pile of books sitting next to her on the cot, and she had a yellow afghan draped over her knees. When she saw me, she peered over the top of her reading glasses. "Oh, it's you! I didn't murder Pete, you know."

"I wasn't going to suggest you had," I said. I held up the box. "I brought you some cinnamon rolls." I turned the box on its side and slid it between the cell bars, and Renee got up and took it with a smile.

"The police seem to think I had a good motive, but really, Pete was never going to succeed in getting the library shut down." Renee sat back down on her cot, already opening the box. She took a big bite of cinnamon roll before adding, "He was a jerk, but not worth murdering. And certainly not worth going to jail for."

I had just been joking with Mama that everyone seemed to be admitting to being a suspect. Renee was my outlier: she was the only person connected to the case who not only downplayed her alleged motive, but she also seemed confident she wouldn't get convicted.

And, right on cue, a police officer walked into the hallway and came to stand next to me. "Okay, Ms. Porter, you're free to go."

Renee put her partially eaten cinnamon roll back into the box. "Great. I'll pack up my things."

I admired how completely unruffled she seemed about the whole ordeal.

The officer unlocked the cell, and I stepped in to help gather up the books while Renee folded her afghan.

"The police should have arrested Pete's wife instead of me," Renee said casually.

"Oh?"

"The two of them would get into the worst shouting matches at the library."

I thought of Fiona's report about hearing Maris and Pete fighting while she was out taking walks. No wonder they had separated. When I said exactly that to Renee, she laughed bitterly. "Oh, it didn't make a difference. They still found excuses to yell at each other all the time. I should have never agreed to let Maris work at the library. Pete would follow her there, and she'd spend half of every shift arguing with him, and the other half pouting in the basement."

Renee breezed past me, out the cell door and toward the reception area. I followed with her pile of books, feeling stunned.

If Maris had worked at the library, then that meant she not only had a motive, but she'd also had the opportunity to lure Pete into the basement, to his death.

CHAPTER ELEVEN

I reminded myself that the police were working with even more information than I had. If they didn't feel like Maris was worth arresting, then neither should I.

Even though I had assured Mama that murder didn't make me that hungry, my stomach was telling a different story after I said goodbye to Renee and walked out of the police station. The day was warm but not hot, and there wasn't a single cloud in the light-blue sky. Already, tourists were making their way toward High Noon Boulevard, and I smiled when I realized many of them were either wearing a Halloween-themed shirt or even decked out in a costume. Cowboy costumes seemed to be the most popular choice, naturally.

I left my car where it was and walked one street over to The Lusty Lunch Counter. It wasn't quite noon yet, but I had decided I could really use a cheeseburger and fries. The Lusty looked like an old diner, complete with over-stuffed red bench seating at the booths and a long stainless steel counter fronted by stools. That, though, was only on the inside.

The clapboard building itself was from Nightmare's Wild West days, and for Halloween, the staff of The Lusty had really leaned into the building's history as a brothel. Up on the rickety balcony above the front door, skeletons had been posed to look like they were waving down at passersby. The skeletons were dressed in corsets, can-can skirts, feather boas, and other accessories that implied they were long-dead ladies of ill repute.

The sexy skeleton theme—at least, that was how I was thinking of it—continued inside. One of the stools at the counter was occupied by a skeleton wearing a cowboy hat and a duster, and a hand of cards had been carefully placed in its bony fingers. A corseted skeleton was posed nearby, one arm raised and the fingers making a *come here* gesture toward the cowboy.

I slid onto a stool, giving the cowboy skeleton a wide berth. My usual server, Ella, wasn't there, and the young man working the counter slid a menu toward me. I was just opening my mouth to tell him I wanted a cheeseburger when I realized it was a special Halloween menu. "I'll have the ground brains burger with zombie sauce," I told him with a laugh.

There was movement to my right while I waited on my renamed cheeseburger, and I looked over to see Maris climbing onto the stool next to me. "Oh, hi," she said, only seeming to realize whom she was sitting next to after getting settled in.

"Can I buy your lunch?" I asked, seeing an opportunity to butter her up. "You've been through an awful lot the past few days."

"No, no," Maris said, waving away the offer. "I don't need any pity, or any money. I was always a better saver than Pete. Plus, I'll have Pete's life insurance payment coming in, and the money from his brother."

"That's kind of your brother-in-law to help you out."

"Help me?" Maris snorted. "He was almost as mean as Pete. But he died over the summer—the cancer really hit him hard, so we knew it was coming, and Pete made sure he was included in his brother's will. The check was mailed just a few weeks ago, to our house in Ohio. I'm going to fly back to get it."

If that check had been mailed in the spring, I realized, it might have been motive for Maris to murder Pete. She'd be rid of her cranky husband, but she would also have some extra money in the bank. Add the life insurance on top of that, and she would have been sitting pretty.

Except, when Pete was murdered, his brother had still been alive.

My cheeseburger arrived, and I ate slowly while my brain sorted through all the details and suspects. Maris didn't seem to mind I wasn't talking to her, because she had a steady stream of people coming by to offer their condolences. As I was standing to go, the person coming over to console Maris was none other than Aaron, the manager of the RV park. He glanced at me, then did a double take.

"Is this lady bothering you?" he asked Maris.

"Not at all." Maris sounded slightly surprised by that fact, as if she had expected me to be a nuisance.

Aaron never said a word to me, but his glare followed me all the way out of the diner. I really hadn't made a good impression by showing up at his RV park to ask probing questions.

My head was still spinning when I got back to my apartment, but I did my best to rest and relax. It was going to be a long afternoon and evening. The family meeting was at three, trick-or-treating through the haunt started at four, and then we would open our doors at seven o'clock for the grownups who wanted to get scared.

In what seemed like no time at all, I was at the Sanctuary, sitting in the dining room. It felt strange to listen to Justine address us when the sun outside the tall windows was still so high in the sky. Mori and Theo weren't there, of course, and I wondered if our two resident vampires were disappointed that they couldn't give out candy, too.

I was delighted when Justine assigned me to the lagoon vignette. Instead of taking tickets, I would get to put on a costume and be a part of the show on the Sanctuary's biggest night of the year.

Shortly before four o'clock, I arrived in the scene that looked like a lagoon, complete with a prop pirate ship that took up a large portion of the space. Seraphina was already in her large glass-fronted water tank, her silver tail flashing as she turned somersaults.

My pirate costume consisted of a long red coat and skirt, a black shirt with lacy cuffs, and tall brown boots. I also had a tricorn hat on my head. When I had changed into the ensemble after the family meeting, I had also been given a burlap sack filled with candy. At a glance, I looked like a pirate who was looting a village.

The first trick-or-treaters came into the lagoon vignette just a few minutes after four. The kids stepped onto the raised wooden walkway, which was designed to look like a boardwalk going over water, and they looked both excited and nervous. When I put a handful of candy into each of their bags, though, any fear they had disappeared, and they said thank you in chorus.

It was adorable.

It was even more adorable when I spotted Lucy walking toward me a couple hours later in her pink dress. Well, maybe walking wasn't the word. She was bouncing along on her toes, making the shimmery fairy wings on her back look like they were flapping.

Clara was holding Lucy's hand, looking nearly as excited as Lucy herself.

Lucy bounded up to me and shouted, "Trick or treat!" Then she turned to her parents, who were following at a more subdued pace. "This is where I played a pirate, too. You should have seen how scary I was!"

I said hi to Nick and Mia while I dropped two handfuls of candy into Lucy's bag. I also gave a piece to Clara, since I knew fairies loved sweets.

As she unwrapped the candy, Clara beamed at Lucy. "Isn't she a fantastic fairy princess?" Lucy didn't know Clara was a real fairy, but Clara was touched by the costume choice, nonetheless.

"Hi, Lucy!" Seraphina called. I looked over to see her at the top of her water tank, her arms resting on the top edge. "Next year, you should be a mermaid for Halloween!"

"I just checked out a book about mermaids at the library," Lucy answered. "I think I should be one, too! Ooh, maybe I could be a mermaid fairy! I could fly *and* swim!"

Lucy, her parents, and Clara moved on to the next scene, and I turned to see what costumes the next group of kids was wearing. Instead, what I saw was Fiona, whose white dress and long black hair were billowing out behind her as she rushed up to me.

"She's here!" Fiona said. "Pete's wife!"

"But why?"

Fiona shrugged. "She's escorting a group of kids. I think the RV park organized the outing for the grandkids of their residents. They do it every year. Anyway, I wanted to give you a heads up. Maybe she'll drop a clue on her way through!"

"Thanks for the tip, Fiona!" I said, but she was already ducking through the hidden door that led to the backstage area of the Sanctuary. That way, she could cut back to her graveyard scene without having to pass any of the trick-or-treaters.

Sure enough, a group of kids walked into the lagoon

vignette about thirty seconds later. Maris was such a short woman that I could barely see her over the heads of the tallest kids, but it was definitely her.

A few of the kids screamed suddenly, and a pair of arms popped up behind them, followed by a face. I started to laugh, then saw it was Aaron doing the scaring. I wondered if he would glare at me again when he realized I was the pirate on duty. At the moment, it was too dim in the vignette, and the group was still too far from where I was standing, for anyone to recognize me.

I tensed as I waited for the group to get closer. When hands suddenly clamped down onto my shoulders, I let out my own shriek of surprise. I turned to see Theo, who was wearing his pirate costume but not his zombie makeup.

"You're up already?" I asked once my heart had returned to a somewhat normal pace. Theo was an expert at sneaking up on me, but I certainly hadn't expected to see him before sundown.

"I wanted to get in on the trick-or-treating," he said, lifting his own burlap sack. "I know how to get from my room to here without having to pass a single window."

"I'm glad you could make it," I told him.

At the same time, I realized the group from the RV park had nearly reached us. I gazed at the group for a few seconds, then gasped as details began to fall into place. All the clues, suspects, and motives that had been spinning through my head settled down as I finally saw the bigger picture.

"Theo," I hissed. I pointed toward Aaron. "Please tackle that man! He killed Pete!"

CHAPTER TWELVE

Theo knew me well enough not to second-guess my instructions. Without a word, he dropped his burlap sack, deftly sidestepped the group of kids, and moved behind Aaron. Before he knew what was happening, Aaron's arms were pinned behind him.

"Where do you want him?" Theo called to me.

"Take him to Damien's office," I said. "Maris, you should join us."

Maris opened her mouth, looking ready to protest, but one look at the expression on Theo's face kept her quiet. After a few moments, though, she said softly, "But what about the kids?"

The kids were staring at Theo and Aaron. They didn't know why the pirate was holding onto one of their chaperones, and the faces that weren't covered by masks showed the beginnings of fear.

To my surprise, it was Malcolm who came to the rescue. He glided out of the shadows, and judging by the bag of candy he was carrying, I figured he had been coming to refill our sacks.

"Not the Halloween trick you were expecting, was it?" Malcolm asked as he bent slightly at the waist and lifted his top hat. He gave the kids his creepiest grin. "I'm going to be your escort now. Do you dare to follow me?"

A couple of the kids giggled, and all of them nodded eagerly. Malcolm was giving them the impression that their chaperones being taken away was all a part of the show.

Aaron and Maris, at least, weren't saying anything to ruin the illusion. Either they were both too shocked or scared to protest, or they realized it was better to discuss the truth of Pete's murder once the kids were out of earshot.

Malcolm moved off with the kids, but only after I gave them candy. I kept a smile on my face, but my fingers were shaking slightly as I plunked the candy into each bag. Once it was just the grownups left, Theo headed for the hidden door, pushing Aaron ahead of him. Maris followed, and I brought up the rear.

Fortunately for Theo, he could also get to Damien's office without encountering any windows. Unfortunately for all of us, we did have to cut through the entryway to get there, which meant a lot of people standing in line saw us. We were giving everyone some fresh gossip.

By the time I followed the others into Damien's office, he was already standing. His eyes caught mine, and I said, "Aaron here killed Pete Bennett."

"Of course I didn't," Aaron protested, craning his neck so he could glare at me.

I knew I wasn't getting through this without him looking at me that way again.

Aaron squirmed, trying to extract his arms from Theo's grip, though it was useless. He was strong but not vampire strong. "You think I killed him just to get revenge for him not paying the fees for his parking pad?"

"No," I said sadly. "I think you killed him to get the money."

Aaron made a noise of incredulity. "What money? You already know Pete didn't pay me for the last six months he was here! He always had an excuse, and he kept promising that if I could just wait a while longer—" Aaron broke off and snapped his mouth shut.

"He kept promising he would have plenty of money soon, didn't he?" I nodded. "His brother had cancer, and the family knew he didn't have much time. Pete told you he'd be getting money from his brother's estate, so if you could overlook the unpaid fees until his brother died, he'd pay every penny he owed."

Aaron gave up his struggle against Theo's grip. "How did you know about that?"

"I didn't, until Maris mentioned it at lunch today. I thought maybe she had killed Pete for the money, but you were the one complaining about being in debt. I realized that whenever I saw Maris, you weren't far away. You broke up her shouting match with Doc outside the saloon, you showed up at the The Lusty today while she was eating there, and now you two are here together. I noticed how closely you and Maris were standing to each other back there, in the lagoon vignette, which is when I realized you're the killer."

Aaron threw a look at Maris. "So me and her are together. That doesn't mean I killed anyone."

"Maris and Pete were separated, but they were still married. It needed to stay that way, so she could get that life insurance payout and the money from her brother-in-law's estate. You put Pete's body in a place it wouldn't be found until the fall. You assumed that, by then, his brother would be dead, and the money would be on its way to Maris and Pete's house in Ohio. If it was known that Pete had died before his brother, there would have been no money from his estate."

Aaron sputtered, then turned his glare to Maris. "Sounds to me like Maris killed him, not me!"

Maris sucked in her breath. "How dare you! You're trying to pin the blame on me?"

"Maris didn't need the money, as she told me herself," I said, loudly enough to be heard over her. "But you did, Aaron. You told Officer Reyes you were struggling to pay for work you got done at the RV park. Instead of getting the money you needed from Pete, you could get it from Maris, just as soon as she cashed the check from her brother-in-law's estate."

Aaron's mouth worked, but no words came out.

"You *wanted* Pete's body to be found," I continued. "Maris would be able to get the life insurance payout without any trouble, and she'd be a widow, so you two could get married. You'd be set financially, and you'd be with Maris."

Maris looked from me to Aaron. "Is it true? You killed Pete just so you could get your hands on the extra money?"

Aaron stared down at the floor. "Yes," he mumbled.

Maris's chest heaved. "You never really loved me, did you? You just pretended to, so I'd share the money with you."

"Of course I loved you! I still do!" Aaron looked at Maris, his anger gone.

Maris shook her head and crossed her arms over her chest. "You just tried to pin the murder you committed on me. That's not love."

Twenty minutes later, Officer Reyes had arrived, and he put Aaron in handcuffs while Maris kept repeating, over and over, that she'd had no idea Aaron had murdered her husband. "I just figured he never called me all summer because he didn't want to talk to me," she said.

It wasn't until the handcuffs were in place that Aaron seemed to realize there was no use protesting his innocence. He told Reyes he had gone into Pete's RV one night, after he had realized eliminating Pete might be the easiest route to getting the money he was owed, and to getting Maris all to himself.

"After I had—you know—I drove Pete's RV to the library, pulled up close to the old coal chute that led into the basement, and slid the body out the door of the RV," Aaron said. "Maris had a key to the library, and I took it when she wasn't looking, so I could get inside and hide the body in the coffin."

Maris made a noise of utter disgust.

"I knew one of the librarians would find him in October, when the Halloween decorations came out," Aaron continued. "Before I put him in the basement, I lopped off his head in the hopes it would buy us some more time before the body was identified. You know, just in case Pete's brother rallied and lived a bit longer than expected."

Maris followed Reyes and Aaron out of Damien's office. By then, the last kids had already gone into the Sanctuary for trick-or-treating, and the entryway queue was beginning to fill up with grown-up guests waiting for the haunt to open at seven.

"Well done, Olivia," Damien said to me. "I'm proud of you."

"Me too," Theo said. He gave me a quick hug. "I'm glad I showed up in time to help you catch the killer. Now, if you'll excuse me, I need to go put on my zombie makeup."

I glanced at my watch, which was hidden under my lacy cuffs. "Wow, I need to get in place! It's ten minutes to seven!"

Damien laughed softly. "Relax, Olivia. Take a little time to process everything that just happened. Go grab a snack in the dining room, or take Felipe outside for a walk."

As if saying his name had summoned him, Felipe appeared in the doorway. He made a snuffling sound, and I took it as his way of agreeing with Damien.

"I have a better idea," I told Damien. "Instead of going outside, why don't you and I walk Felipe inside? I've never liked being the one visiting a haunt, but after the past few days, maybe being scared in a harmless way is exactly what I need." I waved a hand toward Damien. "Come on. It will be fun."

Damien rolled his eyes, but he followed me, anyway. Felipe led the way as we headed to the entryway. I had expected the people waiting in line would complain when they spotted us cutting to the front, but instead, I heard a buzz of approval.

"They just caught Pete Bennett's killer," someone said.

The other comments I heard were of a similar nature, except for the one person who said, "That's a weird-looking dog."

Damien and I waited until seven on the nose before we stepped through the door leading into the haunt. As soon as the door shut behind us, the ghosts of Butch Tanner and Connor McCrory appeared on either side of us, glowing in the darkness. Felipe scampered around them, nipping at their feet but unable to grab the semi-transparent forms with his little fangs.

I could tell Tanner was grinning underneath his red bandana, and he threw his hat into the air. "Let's go!"

McCrory simply said, "We'd be happy to escort the two of you."

"Thank you, gentlemen," I said.

Felipe trotted ahead of our group as we moved forward. Instead of feeling trepidation about going through the haunt, I felt excited. After all, I was with Damien, two ghosts, and a chupacabra. I was safe.

I was home.

As we stepped into the first vignette, Damien looked at me. I could have sworn his green eyes were glowing ever so slightly, but I told myself it must be a trick of the light.

"Happy Halloween, Olivia," he said.

I smiled and reached out to give his hand a squeeze. "It is a very happy Halloween."

A NOTE FROM THE AUTHOR

Thank you for reading *Headless at Halloween*! I love digging into my boxes of Halloween decor every fall, and luckily, I have never found a surprise like the one at the Nightmare Public Library! I hope you had fun with this mystery set during my favorite time of year.

In fact, the inspiration for Nightmare Sanctuary Haunted House came from my wish that I could visit a haunted house attraction at any time of year, instead of having to wait for October to roll around. If you want more Halloween fun, too, you can check out *Halloween Vibes*, a novella in my Eternal Rest Bed and Breakfast paranormal cozy mystery series.

But, before you go, would you please leave a review for *Headless at Halloween*? It really helps other readers find my work. Thank you!

Eternally Yours,

Beth

P.S. You can keep up with my latest book news, get fun freebies, and more by signing up for my newsletter at BethDolgner.com!

MORE HALLOWEEN MYSTERY

Halloween Vibes

ETERNAL REST BED AND BREAKFAST NOVELLA
PARANORMAL COZY MYSTERIES

This Halloween, ghosts are on the case in Oak Hill, Georgia.

Emily Buchanan has always loved Halloween. It's the perfect holiday for welcoming guests to Eternal Rest Bed and Breakfast, but this year, someone is carving up more than jack-o'-lanterns.

When a body is found in the pumpkin patch on the town square, Emily learns the victim's ghost is haunting the crime scene. With the help of her psychic best friend, Sage, Emily will communicate with the victim's ghost to help catch the killer. Along the way, Emily must confront jealous ex-girlfriends and navigate a bitter family rift as she searches for clues.

And Emily really hopes the clues don't point to one of her guests, who had a close tie to the victim.

As Oak Hill transforms from a quaint Southern town into a Halloween haven, Emily must rely on the ghosts of Eternal Rest to help her figure out the truth, all while keeping her guests happy and welcoming a new member of the family to her haunted house…

Halloween Vibes is a standalone novella in the Eternal Rest Bed and Breakfast paranormal cozy mystery series, taking place three months after book seven, Quiet Nights. This series is about hope, determination, and friendship… and solving murders with the help of ghosts in a small town in North Georgia.

ACKNOWLEDGMENTS

I'm so grateful for the team of people who help me get my work out into the world. It begins with my test readers. This time around, it was Kristine, Amber, Alex, and Mom who gave me invaluable feedback. Lia at Your Best Book Editor and Trish at Blossoming Pages polished everything with their editing skills, and Jena at BookMojo gave me a beautiful cover and interior layout. My ARC readers do an incredible job on launch week to top it all off.

ABOUT THE AUTHOR

Beth Dolgner writes paranormal fiction and nonfiction. Her interest in things that go bump in the night really took off on a trip to Savannah, Georgia, so it's fitting that her first series—Betty Boo, Ghost Hunter—takes place in that spooky city. Beth also writes paranormal nonfiction, including her first book, *Georgia Spirits and Specters*, which is a collection of Georgia ghost stories.

Beth and her husband, Ed, live in Tucson, Arizona. They're close enough to Tombstone that Beth can easily visit its Wild West street and watch staged shootouts, all in the name of research for the Nightmare, Arizona series.

Beth also enjoys giving presentations on Victorian death and mourning traditions as well as Victorian Spiritualism. She has been a volunteer at an historic cemetery, a ghost tour guide, and a paranormal investigator.

Keep up with Beth and sign up for her newsletter at
BethDolgner.com.

BOOKS BY BETH DOLGNER

The Nightmare, Arizona Series

Paranormal Cozy Mystery

Homicide at the Haunted House

Drowning at the Diner

Slaying at the Saloon

Murder at the Motel

Poisoning at the Party

Halloween Vibes (Novella)

Clawing at the Corral

Axing at the Antique Store

The Eternal Rest Bed and Breakfast Series

Paranormal Cozy Mystery

Sweet Dreams

Late Checkout

Picture Perfect

Destination Wedding (Novella)

Scenic Views

Breakfast Included

Groups Welcome

Quiet Nights

Halloween Vibes (Novella)

The Betty Boo, Ghost Hunter Series

Romantic Urban Fantasy

Ghost of a Threat

Ghost of a Whisper

Ghost of a Memory

Ghost of a Hope

Manifest

Young Adult Steampunk

A Talent for Death

Young Adult Urban Fantasy

Nonfiction

Georgia Spirits and Specters

Everyday Voodoo

Made in United States
Orlando, FL
14 June 2025

62125138R00059